A Doggie and a Pussycat

How They Were Washing the Floor

Written and drawn by

JOSEF ČAPEK

Prague 2008

Publishing house Baset

Dear children,

Josef Čapek, the writer, wrote for you the Tale About a doggie and a pussycat. For this Tale he also drew lots of very nice pictures. When he was writing and drawing all of this, little Alice was sitting on his lap. She was his daughter and he loved her very much, and little Alice loved her father. Because they were fond of each other like that, Mr. Čapek wrote and drew his story just like his Alice wished. Maybe she even suggested a bit what he should write and draw. However, we are not sure about that, we are just guessing. We would like to tell you that we are in good health and that we just began to be published as a serial for children. Now, as far as we know, you are going to be told in different books how we were washing the floor, how we made a cake, how we were writing a letter, how doggie tore his pants, then about a doll which was crying faintly and also about a proud night shirt. We are looking forward to tell you more. We hope that you feel the same. So bye and regards,

Yours PUSSYCAT and DOGGIE

It was in those days when the doggie and the pussycat were still keeping a house together; they had their little house and there they lived with each other near the forest.

They used to do something well, and something not so well; so one day they noticed that there is a very dirty floor in their little house.

"Just take a look", said the doggie, "my paws are grubby because of this dirty floor."
"We have to wash the floor," said the pussycat.

"Well, you go and get the water and I will take care of the rest." So the doggie went with a saucepan to bring some water.

The pussycat took a piece of soap from her suitcase and put the soap down on the table.

Then she went for something to the larder, since she probably had a slice of smoked mouse hidden there. She liked that a lot.

Meanwhile the doggie came back with the water and saw something lying on the table.

He unwrapped it and saw it was pink. "Hullo, that must be something tasteful," said the doggie.

Since he wanted to eat it so much he put that whole piece into his mouth and started to munch and crunch it.

Then the pussycat came back and heard how the doggie was sputtering strangely.

She looked at him and saw that the doggie's muzzle was full of foam and tears were running from his eyes.

"Good heavens!" the pussycat cried out, "what happened to you, doggie? Froth is dripping from your mouth! What is happening to you?!"

"Well, I found something on the table and I thought that it could be some cheese or some sweet, so I ate it," said the doggie.

"Oh, you are so foolish," the pussycat was angry. "It's soap! And soap is used for washing, of course, not for eating!"

"Drink a lot of water," suggested the pussycat to the doggie, "then it will stop biting your tongue." The doggie took a drink so big that he drunk all the water.

Then he went to dry his muzzle on the grass, and then had to go to get water again because he drunk it all and they had none left.

The pussycat had one crown and she went to buy a new soap.

"This one I won't eat again," said the doggie when the pussycat returned with the new soap.

Then she took the soap and a saucepan full of water, knelt on the floor, took the doggie as a scrubbing brush, and scrubbed the floor with the doggie.

"Now we should wipe it up with something dry," said the pussycat, because the floor was completely wet and it wasn't very clean as yet.

"Well, now I will take you and dry the floor with you," said the doggie.
He took the pussycat and wiped the whole floor with her.

Both the doggie and the pussycat were completely wet and awfully dirty from washing the floor with each other.

"We will wash ourselves just like we wash our clothes," the doggie said.
They filled a washtub with water and took a scrubbing board as well.

Then the doggie climbed into the water and the pussycat washed him properly. She was scrubbing him so hard that his legs almost tangled.

When the doggie was clean, the pussycat climbed into the washtub and
the doggie washed her. He pressed so hard that he almost rubbed out
a hole in her fur.

Then they wrung each other out. "And now we will dry ourselves," said the pussycat. They prepared the clotheslines.

The doggie took the pussycat and hung her on the line just like the clothes get hanged. After that the pussycat got down and hung up the doggie.

And so both of them were hanging there and the sun was shining on them happily. "The sun is shining on us," said the doggie, "we are going to be dry soon."

As soon as he said that it started to rain. "It's raining!" cried out
the doggie and the pussycat, "our clothes will get wet." And they ran
into the house to hide under the roof.

"Is it still raining?" asked the pussycat. "It stopped already," the doggie replied and the sun really was shining again.

"So we will hang our clothes again," the pussycat said. So they went and hung themselves on the line again.

And it started to rain again. "It's raining, our clothes will get wet!" shouted the doggie and the pussycat and again ran to hide themselves.

Then the sun was shining once more and so they both hung each other on the line all over again.

And then it was raining again so they ran away, and then the sun was shining again so they hung each other again.

This was going on until the evening came, but they were both completely dry by then. "The clothes are dry now," they said to each other, "so we will put them in a basket."

So they climbed into the basket, but then began to feel tired so they fell asleep there, and both slept beautifully in the basket until the morning.

Dear children,

in our next story you will find out, how be made a cake. We are offering you
a few pictures from the story to color in. When your parents buy you the book, you
will find out, if you colored it in correctly.

Yours PUSSYCAT and DOGGIE

Already published:

  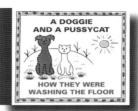 

A Doggie and a Pussycat

How They Were Washing the Floor

Eduard Hofman adapted the story and pictures by Josef Čapek, it was drawn by Josef Tokstein. Adapted from an animated movie by Eduard Hofman on motives by Josef Čapek.
Translation: Jaroslav Vydra
Graphical layout and typesetting: Radim Prokop
Printing and binding: Tisk a vazba: PBtisk s.r.o.
Publishing house Miloš Uhlíř - Baset, Prague, Czech Republic, 2008
ISBN 80-7340-018-9

Publishing house Baset
Plovdivská 3400, 143 00 Praha 4 - Modřany
telefon/fax: +420 244 402 706
e-mail: baset@ok.cz
www.baset.cz